Aziza's
·Secret Fairy·
Door
and the Magic Puppy

Other books by Lola Morayo

Aziza's Secret Fairy Door and the Magic Puppy

Lola Morayo

Illustrated by Cory Reid

MACMILLAN CHILDREN'S BOOKS

With special thanks to Tọ́lá Okogwu

Published 2023 by Macmillan Children's Books
an imprint of Pan Macmillan
The Smithson, 6 Briset Street, London EC1M 5NR
EU representative: Macmillan Publishers Ireland Ltd, 1st Floor,
The Liffey Trust Centre, 117–126 Sheriff Street Upper
Dublin 1, D01 YC43
Associated companies throughout the world
www.panmacmillan.com

ISBN 978-1-5290-6401-8

Text copyright © Storymix Limited 2023
Illustrations copyright © Cory Reid 2023
Series created by Storymix Limited.
Edited by Jasmine Richards.

The right of Storymix Limited and Cory Reid to be identified as the
author and illustrator of this work has been asserted by them
in accordance with the Copyright, Designs and Patents Act 1988.

1 3 5 7 9 8 6 4 2

A CIP catalogue record for this book is available from the British Library.

Printed and bound by CPI Group (UK) Ltd, Croydon CR0 4YY

MIX
Paper | Supporting
responsible forestry
FSC® C116313

For Goziam.

My life with you is the greatest adventure yet!

T. O.

To Ṭọlá and Cory, what an adventure it has been!

You are both MAGIC!

J. R.

Pre moju Wifeček. L'úbim t'a!

C. R.

Chapter 1

'But my friend Jola has a dog.' Otis put down his fork and crossed his arms.

Aziza saw her dad share a look with Mum across the dinner table. Dad then sighed deeply. 'We've been through this, Otis.'

'The flat is too small,' Mum added with a sympathetic smile. 'You wouldn't want the dog to feel all cooped up, would you? Dogs need lots of space.'

Aziza pushed a piece of fried plantain around her plate. She'd lost count of the number of times her brother had begged their

parents for a pet. But the answer was always the same.

'I could make room. And we have the balcony,' Otis pleaded. 'I'd take it out for a walk every day so it wouldn't feel all cooped up.'

'I'd help too,' Aziza offered.

'I'm sorry, kids. We're also not allowed big pets in the flat,' Dad said. 'How about a goldfish instead? They're cute.'

'A goldfish?' Otis exclaimed with a horrified expression. 'They're not cute. They're boring. You can't teach them tricks or take them for walks.'

Aziza secretly agreed, but she knew better than to get involved in this argument. *It's not like it's Mum and Dad's fault we can't get a dog.*

Otis pushed his plate of half-finished food away. 'It's just not fair,' he muttered under his breath.

Dad shared another look with Mum but she just shook her head with a sad smile.

The rest of dinner went quietly. When they were finished, Mum asked Aziza and Otis to clear the table.

'You know what, Otis,' Aziza said as she stacked the plates, 'maybe a goldfish wouldn't be so bad?'

Otis's face creased into an annoyed frown. 'You're right. Having a goldfish wouldn't be bad – it would be terrible. I want a dog.'

'I was just . . .'

'Just leave it,' Otis interrupted. 'You wouldn't understand. All you care about are those pretend fairies.'

Aziza gasped. 'That's not very nice.'

Otis looked down but still wore a stubborn expression on his face.

'Fine,' Aziza said, putting the plate in her hand down. 'You can finish cleaning up by yourself then.'

Aziza walked away. Out of the corner of her eye she thought she saw her brother looking a bit guilty, but she couldn't be sure.

★

Aziza shut her bedroom door with a soft click. *It's not my fault Otis can't have a pet*, she thought. *Why is he taking it out on me?*

Tick, tock, tick, tock.

Aziza paused. She didn't have a ticking clock in her room. She turned towards the sound. It was coming from the fairy door that sat on her windowsill. The door was covered in tiny spring blossoms and green leaves.

She rushed over to it, forgetting all about Otis and their argument. The tick, tocking got louder and the doorknob was glowing. Aziza reached for it and felt a shiver of anticipation race through her body. *I'm going back to the magical world of Shimmerton!* she thought. *I'll get to see Peri and Tiko again!* The fairy door opened, bathing Aziza in a golden beam of light. However, just as she stepped through, her bedroom door crashed open with a loud bang. Aziza whipped around.

'I'm sorry, Zizi,' Otis began. 'I didn't mean

to—Whoa!' he exclaimed. 'What's going on here?'

Otis's dark brown eyes were super wide.

Uh-oh, Aziza thought. She was the only one in her world who knew about the magic of the fairy door. *Not any more*, Aziza realized.

Aziza opened her mouth to explain, but she could feel herself shrinking as she got pulled through the door.

'Wait! Where are you going?' Otis raced towards her. Aziza saw the fairy door's golden beam cover him too, and then he was pulled through the doorway with her.

Soon they were through to the other side. Aziza and Otis stared at each other as they found themselves on a cobbled path, surrounded by rolling green hills.

'That whole door thing was awesome,' Otis said. 'But I have some questions.'

'So do I,' Aziza responded. 'Why did you follow me?'

'You're my sister, Aziza,' Otis explained patiently. 'What kind of big brother would let you go through some strange magical door by yourself? Now we just need to figure out what's going on.'

Aziza raised an eyebrow. 'Maybe I know what's going on.'

Otis looked surprised and then grinned. 'You do? Spill the beans.' He looked around.

Aziza saw his mouth drop open as he took in the pink sky, swirled with candy-floss coloured clouds, and the jewel-toned shops that lined Shimmerton's high street in the distance. 'They eat beans here, right?' Otis added.

Aziza smiled, remembering how amazing it had felt the first time she came through the fairy door. 'They eat beans and lots of other cool things as well,' she reassured him.

'Where are we?' Otis looked back at the closed fairy door. Its edges were already blending into the side of the flagstone wall. 'The door's disappeared!'

'It does that,' Aziza replied. Her dungarees had been replaced by a simple pair of jeans and a short-sleeve, patterned top. It was covered in tiny flowers that complemented the butterfly wings that now sprouted from her back. 'We're in the magical kingdom of Shimmerton,' Aziza added.

'It's incredible,' Otis whispered in awe. 'How many times have you been here?'

'Quite a few,' Aziza admitted. 'The first time I came through was the day I got the fairy door.'

'No wonder you've been so into fairies,'

Otis said. 'I mean, more than usual. You've been hiding this the whole time.' Otis turned around, trying to get a better look at their surroundings. His top rippled with magical colour.

'Hey, you've got wings too!' Aziza gasped, spying a silvery set of dragonfly wings flickering behind him.

'YES!' Otis exclaimed, spinning on the spot and trying to get a better look. 'Oooh, I'm going to fly.' He wriggled his shoulders and leapt into the air. But he dropped straight back down again.

'They don't work!' Otis grumbled. His top flashed red. 'What's wrong with them?'

'It takes a lot of practice,' Aziza explained as she fluttered her own. 'It took Peri ages to teach me.'

'Who's Peri?'

Aziza smiled. She was actually really loving that her brother was here. 'She's my friend. She's also the princess of Shimmerton, but she's not a big fan of princess dresses or doing the other boring things that come with the job. Then there's Tiko, he's a shape-shifter. He's super sweet and brave.'

Otis stared at Aziza in amazement. His top turned yellow. 'A shape-shifter?'

'You'll see.' Aziza grabbed her brother's arm. 'There are so many magical creatures that live here. I can't wait for you to meet them all.'

'It doesn't seem like *anybody* lives here,' Otis said with a doubtful look around.

Aziza followed his gaze. Otis was right. There was no one on the path or on the high street. *Glittersticks! Where is everybody?* Aziza thought.

'Wait a sec,' Otis said, pointing to a small sign just up ahead. 'I think that's our answer.'

Aziza went over to get a closer look. Otis followed close behind her.

This way to the spring fete
→

The letters were written in gold paint and beneath them an arrow pointed towards the high street.

'Of course!' Aziza said, clapping her hands. 'They must all be at the fete. Let's go find Peri and Tiko.'

Chapter 2

They arrived at the village fete to find the Princess of Shimmerton stamping her foot at the hoopla stand. In her hand, Peri held a wooden hoop. Beside her stood her bear-like best friend, with an anxious expression on his face. Aziza could tell that Peri hadn't spotted them yet – her gaze was fixed on the stall in front of her and the minotaur that stood behind it. Two thick horns rose from either side of his head in a fearsome display. The ground around him was littered with coloured hoops and Aziza soon saw why. The wooden hoop left Peri's hand and sailed through the air, missing the minotaur completely.

'Come on, Princess,' he chuckled deeply. 'You can do better than that.'

Tiko's nose began to twitch with worry. 'Why don't you try throwing it gently?

You could really hurt someone.'

'I am throwing it gently!' Peri muttered through gritted teeth. She picked up another hoop, reached back and flung it through the air. It whizzed past the minotaur, landing beside a startled goblin in the next stall.

'This game isn't fair,' Peri insisted with a flap of her swan-like wings. 'He won't sit still.' The minotaur chuckled again.

'What about the strength tester game instead?' Aziza called out. 'You'd be good at that since you're so strong.'

Peri and Tiko swivelled around, their

frowns melting away when they spotted Aziza.

'Aziza!' Peri squealed and pulled her into a big hug.

'You came,' Tiko said. 'I really hoped you would.'

'The spring fete is totally the coolest day of the year,' Peri added. 'We get to skip school and play games all day.' Peri paused as she spotted Otis.

'This is my brother, Otis,' Aziza said quickly.

Otis grinned. 'Hey there!'

Tiko took his hand and shook it firmly. 'We've heard so much about you and how much you love the superhero Jamal Justice.'

Otis looked a bit shy. 'Well, our parents did invent him.'

'We know all about it,' Peri declared. 'Jamal has a Ray Atomizer and he fights for justice.'

Aziza squirmed as Peri talked about the superhero star of their parents' graphic novels. She could tell Otis felt embarrassed.

'Have you checked out any other stalls yet?' Tiko asked.

Otis shook his head. 'Aziza wanted to find you first.'

'In that case, come on.' Peri grabbed his arm. 'The roulette raffle stall is next door.'

They hurried to an adjacent stall where Mr Bracken the unicorn was busy adjusting a giant wheel. The wheel was divided into sparkly sections numbered from one to ten.

'Is that unicorn wearing a tank top—' Otis began.

Aziza elbowed him quickly. 'Hi, Mr Bracken.'

'Good to see you again, young lady,' the unicorn replied. 'Would you like to have a go?' Mr Bracken pointed to the wheel.

'I don't know how to play.'

'It's easy!' Peri cried. 'The wheel is magical. You just pick a number between one and ten. If the wheel calls out your number, you win a prize.'

Mr Bracken coughed. 'Aren't you forgetting something?'

'Oh yeah,' Peri said with a sheepish grin. 'The wheel decides who it thinks deserves to win.'

Otis scratched his head. 'So the wheel is kind of alive?'

Peri shrugged 'Nah — it's just magic. It's hard to explain. It's a Shimmerton thing!'

'Ok, then. I choose number four,' Otis said.

'Eight,' Aziza added.

Peri grinned and picked her number, followed by Tiko. Mr Bracken spun the wheel.

'Hold on, we haven't had a go!' announced a high-pitched voice.

Not the Gigglers, Aziza thought, as Kendra, Felly and Noon pushed their way in front of the stall.

'I love roulette raffle,' exclaimed Noon.

The pink-haired fairy clapped her hands.

'Me too,' said Felly, fluttering her moth wings.

'Would you both be quiet,' Kendra hissed. 'I'm trying to pick a number.'

Mr Bracken snorted. 'Well, hurry up then. The wheel can't be stopped once it starts counting.'

The Gigglers chose their numbers quickly and, almost immediately, a loud voice rang out.

'One . . . six . . . nine . . .'

Kendra nudged Felly. 'Look, it sounds just like you when you're counting.'

'That's well rude,' Felly complained. 'It's okay that it takes me a while to work stuff out.'

'Yeah, Kendra,' Noon added. 'You get your nines and sixes mixed up too.'

Soon the Gigglers were arguing and Aziza sighed. *This is so typical of them. I bet one of them will win too, knowing my luck.*

As the wheel slowed down, so did the counting, until at last it called out its final number – 'Four!'

'I won,' Otis squealed.

Aziza was happy for Otis, but she couldn't

help but feel disappointed. *Of course Otis would win something the very first time he's in Shimmerton. Why did the wheel choose him?*

'That's not fair,' Felly cried.

'He only just got here,' Noon whined.

'Hold on ... who is he?' Kendra demanded.

'He's Aziza's brother,' Peri replied. Aziza could tell Peri was enjoying the Gigglers' annoyance.

Kendra eyed Aziza up and down. 'Is your whole family moving into Shimmerton now?'

'What will it be, young man?' Mr Bracken

asked. 'I have some magic toy soldiers, or perhaps you'd like your own hot-air balloon.'

'What about that magic fairy puppy?' Kendra cried, pointing to a small basket in the corner. 'That would make the perfect prize.'

A puppy? Aziza followed Kendra's finger and saw a puppy with white fur and the biggest, most adorable eyes. His tiny fairy wings were flapping excitedly. *Oh no!*

'What about the toy soldiers?' Aziza suggested quickly.

But Otis wasn't listening, his attention fixed on the puppy.

'Otis—,' Aziza began in warning, 'you can't have the—'

'Puppy,' Otis cried. 'I'll take the puppy.'

The Gigglers cheered.

'But Otis,' Aziza said, 'you don't know how to look after a regular dog, never mind a fairy one.'

Otis snorted. 'How much harder could it be? I just need to feed him, play with him and take him for walks. Easy.'

'Good choice, but do watch out,' Mr Bracken warned, lifting the puppy out. 'This puppy has a bark like thunder and it's definitely worse than his bite.' He placed the puppy in Otis's arms. 'If you decide he's too much to handle you can bring him back and I'll find him the perfect home.'

'No way,' Otis exclaimed as he scratched the top of the puppy's head. 'You're not going to be a problem. Are you little guy?'

The puppy nuzzled his hand then gave it a big lick. Otis laughed and Aziza sighed. *'There's no way he's bringing that puppy back,'* she muttered under her breath. Then she realised that the Gigglers were staring at her.

'What?'

Kendra smirked. 'Are you *sure* you two are related?'

Aziza frowned. 'Yeah, why?'

'Clearly he got all the fun genes.'

Noon and Felly started giggling and even Otis laughed.

'That's not funny.' Aziza frowned at her brother. Why was he siding with the Gigglers?

'It sort of is. Cheer up, Zizi, it's just a joke.'

'Yeah, Zizi.' Kendra smirked. 'We're only joking.'

'What are you going to call him?' Tiko asked, stepping between Aziza and the Gigglers.

'What about Pogo?' Tiko suggested.

'Boring! How about Kendra?' suggested Kendra.

Peri rolled her eyes. 'You can't name him after yourself.'

'Why not?' Kendra asked. 'It's a brilliant name.'

Otis thought for a minute. His top, which had been changing colours, settled on blue. 'I'm calling him Hainu.'

'What kind of name is that?' Kendra scoffed.

Otis shrugged defensively. 'It's a winged dog I read about in a comic book once. I like it.' Otis bent and scratched the puppy on the head again. 'You do too, don't you Hainu?'

The puppy leapt into Otis's arms, and butted his soft head against Otis's cheek. *I guess he likes it*, Aziza thought. *He's so cute, maybe he won't be too difficult to look after.*

At that very moment, Hainu's head pricked up, and with a mighty leap, he surged out of Otis's arms.

'Hainu!' Otis called, but the puppy had already flown into the minotaur's stall.

The minotaur squealed when he saw the dog and jumped onto his stool. But Hainu kept going, dashing past him and towards the ice cream stall.

Mrs Sayeed was serving a pixie a nettle-leaf ice cream. She shook her head at the puppy, her glistening horn catching the spring sunshine. 'This ice cream isn't for fairy doggies.'

There was a flash of white fur as Hainu darted off again, disappearing into the crowd.

'I can't see him,' Otis cried, as they passed an ogre and its pet porcupine who were trying to guess the weight of the moonbeam hanging from the stall.

Aziza groaned. 'I told you a magic puppy was a bad idea.'

'Oi,' shouted a gruff voice, 'Watch out!'

Chapter 3

Aziza jumped out of the way just as a large,

spotted egg rolled past. It was followed

by a tall troll. Close behind him, a small

unicorn struggled with an oversized egg,

almost as big as him. Aziza recognized

Fern, Mr Bracken's nephew.

'It's an egg rolling competition,' Otis cried as they tried to edge past. 'Doesn't seem very fair, though.'

Aziza nodded just as Officer Alf appeared, pointing frantically at some orange safety cones.

'Please go around,' he huffed. 'Can't you see there's a race in progress?'

Several Shimmerton residents dashed past, including a goblin and a faun. Aziza even spotted Mr Phoenix the pharmacist hobbling along beside Mrs Hattie, the sphinx. *There's something very odd-looking about them*, Aziza thought. *Glittersticks! It's a three-legged race.*

Suddenly, Mr Phoenix tripped on Mrs Hattie's long tail and they tumbled forward. Unable to stop in time, the pairs of runners behind them also stumbled, collapsing into a small heap on the ground.

'This race is a complete hazard,' Officer Alf declared, waving his elf and safety clipboard in the air. 'I told you three legs is a bad idea.'

'Speak for yourself,' screeched a three-legged crow. Its pitch-black feathers gleamed as it soared past the pile of racers

and straight across the finish line.

'Look!' Tiko pointed to the spinning tea cup café that had set up a little stall. 'There's Hainu.'

By the time they reached him, Hainu was zipping between the giant teacups. It took ages to catch the puppy, who had three strange-looking sticks in his mouth.

'That was naughty,' Otis scolded, gathering Hainu in his arms. The puppy wagged his tail and kept gnawing on the sticks.

Aziza couldn't help but laugh. *He must really like sticks,* she thought. She leant over to get a better look. The bark on each stick was a different colour. Gold, silver and bronze. Each thicker than the last. *Where on earth did he get those from?*

Before Aziza could ask, a bell rang loudly

through the air. *Clang, clang, clang.*

'Oh no! It's midday already,' Peri groaned. 'I promised my parents I wouldn't be late!'

'Late for what?' Otis asked.

'The unveiling of the town clock,' Tiko replied. 'Every year the Zorigami restores it as part of the Spring celebration.'

'What's a Zorigami?' Otis asked, as he tried to pull one of the sticks from Hainu's mouth.

'A clock that came to life on its thousandth birthday. The town clock is ancient, so the Zorigami has to use special materials from all over Shimmerton to keep it running.'

'The whole ceremony is proper boring,' Kendra added, strolling up to join them along with Felly and Noon.

'It's important,' Tiko insisted. 'The clock represents spring and growth. Without it, nothing would grow.'

'Come on,' Peri said, pointing to the growing crowd. 'If we hurry, we can still make it.'

Tiko, Peri and Aziza raced towards the clock. Otis and the Gigglers followed but they were slower because they kept stopping to play with Hainu, who had wriggled out of Otis's arms again. By the time Aziza, Peri and Tiko arrived, the king and queen were waiting with an impatient-looking Zorigami. The clock-creature was tapping his wooden foot. Peri mouthed an apology to her parents from where she stood. It looked like almost everyone from Shimmerton was already there, but the town clock was still covered in the velvet cloth.

There was a buzz of excitement as the Zorigami reached for the cloth. He removed it with a flourish and a loud gasp erupted from the crowd, followed by a terrible silence.

'What's wrong?' Aziza asked.

'The three hands on the clock are missing,' Peri whispered back. 'I'd better go and see if I can help.' She ran towards the stage.

'What happened to my beautiful clock?' tick-tocked the Zorigami. 'It's been vandalized.'

'Oh dear,' Tiko said, his nose twitching fiercely. 'This is very bad indeed.'

A low murmur spread through the crowd. The queen handed the Zorigami a brown paper bag to breathe into as he had begun to hyperventilate.

'Everything okay?' Otis asked as he, the Gigglers and Hainu finally joined Aziza and her friends. He pulled the sticks from the puppy's mouth.

Aziza shook her head. 'Not really, the hands of the clock are miss—'

'Hey, I know,' Otis interrupted. 'Let's play fetch.' Otis offered the three sticks to the Gigglers. 'You can have one each.'

Aziza shook her head in disbelief. Since when was her brother such great pals with the Gigglers?

'I'm brilliant at fetch,' Felly said.

'It's the puppy doing the fetching, not you,' Noon replied.

Otis laughed. 'You are funny, Felly.' He gave a stick to each Giggler. The Gigglers pulled their arms back, ready to hurl the twigs and Hainu snapped to attention, ready to play. A flash of light from the sticks caught Aziza's attention. *Hang on*, she thought. *There's three missing clock hands. There's three*

sticks. Those aren't twigs. They're . . .

'WAIT,' bellowed the Zorigami. 'Whatever you do, don't throw those sticks!'

But as usual, the Gigglers weren't paying any attention. They sent the sticks flying. Aziza watched as the first stick landed on the ground and disappeared in a shower of sparkles. The second and the third soon followed. It was as if they'd never even been there.

'Whatever have you done?' The Zorigami cried, running up to them. Peri was by his side. 'Do you know how much work it took to source those clock hands?'

'But they're just sticks,' Kendra protested.

'And I'm just a clock,' the Zorigami muttered. 'Don't you know those sticks are magical? Once they land on the ground they return to where they came from.'

'Can't you just magic up some new ones?' asked Noon.

'Younglings,' the Zorigami snorted. 'You think everything is so quick and easy. It's taken me all year to find those sticks.'

'Oh dear,' Tiko whispered.

'I'm sorry,' Otis said. 'Hainu is my puppy and he had the sticks. I should have taken better care of him.'

Aziza stepped closer to her brother. 'We all should have. We really are sorry.'

Peri straightened. 'We'll get them back so you can repair the clock.'

'We promise,' Tiko added.

'Too right you will, and you'd better get a move on,' the Zorigami tick-tocked. 'Time waits for no one. You have until sunset to find the sticks or nothing will come into spring this year and Shimmerton will be ruined.'

'Nothing?' Otis breathed, a worried look on his face.

'It's really simple. Spring will pause until the clock is fixed. You don't have long. Are you sure you want to spend your time talking to me?'

Aziza swallowed as a new thought occurred to her. *If spring in Shimmerton is paused, does that mean the fairy door won't work?*

'What's the matter, Zizi?' Otis asked. 'You look a bit sick.'

'I don't know for sure,' said Aziza, 'but I think we won't be able to get home until we fix that clock.'

Chapter 4

'We can't be stuck,' Otis cried. 'What about Mum and Dad?'

Aziza nodded. She didn't want to be stuck in Shimmerton forever either. *As much as I love it here, I'd miss Mum and Dad too much.*

'It's okay, they won't even know we're gone. Time here moves differently from in our world, Otis, but I don't think the magic of the fairy door will work until time starts moving forward again.'

'We need to fix that clock so we can get home.' Otis looked determined.

Tiko patted Aziza on the shoulder. 'Don't worry. We'll help you.'

'Yeah,' Peri said. 'We'll do it together.'

From the corner of her eye, Aziza saw Kendra, Felly and Noon edging away. *Typical.*

Tiko turned to the Zorigami. 'Where have the clock hands travelled back to?'

'The bronze second hand comes from the Wailing Woods. You'll find the silver minute hand up on Ice Mountain, and the golden hour hand was originally found in Shimmerton's main river.'

'That doesn't sound too difficult,' Peri said eagerly.

'Younglings!' huffed the Zorigami. 'You HAVE to collect them in the right order. That's vital, otherwise the clock won't work. Second hand, then minute hand and lastly the hour hand. Did you get that?'

Aziza noticed Otis, who'd spotted the Gigglers edging away.

'Aren't you going to help?' Otis asked.

'Nah,' Kendra replied. 'Sounds like a lot of work and there's still tons of stalls we haven't visited.'

'But you threw the sticks. You have to help,' Otis insisted.

Kendra raised an eyebrow. 'Wasn't it your puppy who stole them in the first place?'

'B-but—,' Otis stuttered.

'Yeah,' Felly interrupted. 'Sounds like you're a very irresponsible pet owner.'

Kendra beat her shiny beetle wings and flew up into the air. 'Besides, you lot seem to have everything in order.'

Felly and Noon also took flight and the three fairies glided away.

Otis stared after the Gigglers. 'I can't

believe they just left like that.'

Peri shrugged. 'They're the Gigglers. It's
what they do.'

'Don't worry, Otis,' Aziza said. 'We don't need them.'

Peri put her hands on her hips. 'So, where to first?'

'We need to get the bronze second hand first,' Aziza said.

Tiko nodded. 'The Zorigami said it was in the Wailing Woods.'

Peri tapped her chin. 'We'll have to fly if we're going to get everything in time.'

Otis's face lit up. 'Yes! I've been waiting for this. I'm sure I'll be able to do it this time.'

Otis tried to take off, but his wings only gave

the littlest flutter and his feet barely left the ground. 'It's not working.'

Aziza moved closer to her brother. 'I can teach you how to fly if you want?'

Otis kicked a stone with his foot. 'What's the point? I'm rubbish at it.'

Aziza shrugged. 'You just need a little practice. I wasn't very good when I first started.'

'Really?' Otis started to smile. 'You're not messing with me?'

Aziza nodded. 'First rule of flying – it's all about your shoulders,' Aziza pulled her arms to her side and moved her shoulders up and down. 'Copy me.'

'Like this?' Otis replied, with a few big shrugs. Hainu wiggled his front paws too.

Aziza smiled. 'That's it.'

Otis grinned back. 'What next?'

'This bit should be easy for you. Let go of all your worries,' Aziza said. 'Think about how amazing it would feel to be in the air right now.'

Otis closed his eyes and wrapped his arms tighter around Hainu. A peaceful expression came over his face.

'Brilliant,' Aziza said. 'Let that positive energy flow through your whole body, right to the tips of your wings. Can you feel the warmth?'

Suddenly Otis's feet lifted off the ground. He was so surprised he let go of Hainu. The puppy seemed to fall for a moment before his wings took over and he righted himself.

'Whoa!' Otis cried as he sailed through the air with Hainu in tow, his wings flapping hard.

'That's it, Otis,' Aziza called from down below. 'You're doing it. I knew you could!'

Peri nudged Aziza. 'Nice one.'

Aziza smiled. 'I had a great teacher.'

Then she took a deep breath. *Time to find my own happy thought.* She pictured Otis's happy face as he soared into the sky. Then with a wiggle of her shoulders, Aziza shot up too, Peri close behind her.

'You coming or what, Tiko?' Peri shouted down.

Tiko shut his eyes and scrunched his nose in concentration. With a flash of sparkles, Tiko's furry body disappeared, replaced instead by a strange-looking bird.

'Erm, Tiko,' Peri asked. 'Why did you turn into a chicken? They can't fly.'

'I'm not a chicken,' Tiko squawked. 'I'm a Sarimanok.'

He stretched his multicoloured wings wide and flapped, joining his friends in the air. Together they raced towards the Wailing Woods.

From the air, Aziza soon spotted the familiar

stretch of dark forest. It unfolded below them – gnarled trees covering the grassy plains like a thick, dense beard. Aziza, Otis and their friends landed near the edge of woods.

'This place looks properly scary,' Otis
murmured as he gazed at the path winding
through the dark forest.

Suddenly, a low wail echoed through the

twisting trees in a haunting melody.

'Did that come from in there?' Otis whispered.

Peri nodded. 'It's why it's called the Wailing Woods. It's the wind through the trees.'

'I still don't like this place,' Tiko muttered, now back to his usual self.

'It's OK,' Aziza said. She took a confident step onto the path. 'Come on guys. We need

to search the forest floor. We can do this together.'

The others followed slowly through the sun-dappled forest. Plants and trees stretched towards the soft light that streamed through their twisted branches, breaking into a kaleidoscope of colours. Dew drops glistened on the tiny buds peeking from the green stems.

'This place will be so beautiful once

it's properly spring,' Otis said.

Aziza bit her lip. 'Only if we fix the clock in time.'

Peri slowed her steps. 'Imagine if the flowers don't open in the palace gardens. My mum will be devastated.'

But Aziza had realized something even worse. *What will happen to the bees and other insects that need the nectar and pollen from those flowers?*

'Let's hurry,' Aziza said, striding determinedly ahead, searching the forest floor. 'We don't have much time.'

Hainu scampered ahead and soon returned

with a small stick in his mouth.

'Look, he's found a stick!' Otis exclaimed. 'He's trying to help.'

Aziza smiled. 'Are you sure he's not just wanting another game of fetch?'

Otis patted Hainu's head. 'Don't listen to her.' He pulled the brown stick from Hainu's mouth. 'Nice try, boy.' Then he threw the stick and the puppy dashed off after it.

They all carried on looking, but after a while Peri stopped with a sigh.

'This isn't working, and we're running out of time'

'There are so many sticks,' Otis grumbled, 'and none of them are the right one.'

'It might help if Hainu stopped playing with every single one,' Peri muttered.

Otis frowned. 'Hey, it's not his fault.'

'Well actually . . .'

'Why don't we visit Duende?' Aziza suggested before Peri could finish her sentence. 'I think we all need something to drink and

Duende might be able to give us some advice on finding the bronze stick.'

'That's a brilliant idea.' Tiko replied.

'What or who is Duende?' Otis asked.

'He's a very nice elf that lives in these woods,' Aziza replied, throwing the stick away. 'He's also really good at whistling.'

'So how do we find him?' Otis asked.

'That's easy,' Aziza said with a smile. 'Just follow your nose.'

Aziza demonstrated by taking a deep breath. Almost immediately the warm scent of spices filled her nostrils.

Otis took a big sniff too. 'I can smell
something,' he exclaimed. 'It smells like
cinnamon.'

'And nutmeg,' Peri added.

'There,' Tiko cried, pointing to a shaft of orange light that cut through the forest. 'It's Duende's cave.'

Chapter 5

The inside of the cave was snug and cosy.
Scented candles lit up the whole room and
beside a roaring fire sat an elf-like creature
with pointy ears and an equally pointy nose.
In his lap was a book.

'Duende,' Tiko called in greeting.

Duende looked up with a startled expression. 'Why, Tiko, it's so good to see you again.' Then he spotted the others. 'All of you. Would you like a drink, or perhaps something to eat? I have some moss crisps.'

At the sight of food, Hainu jumped up excitedly.

'I'll take that as a yes then,' Duende said with a smile.

After they'd settled in front of the fire with their hot drinks and crisps, and Aziza had properly introduced Otis to Duende, she explained all about the town clock and the missing sticks.

'If we don't find the sticks before the sun sets everything will stay stuck and spring will be ruined,' she finished.

Duende's face fell. 'That's terrible. The woods just wouldn't be the same without spring.'

Aziza shivered and rubbed her arms as she thought again about herself and Otis being stuck in Shimmerton forever.

'Oh, you're getting cold.' Duende reached for a small basket of wood and grabbed some kindling. 'I'll just add more wood to the fire.'

Suddenly, Peri sprung up from her chair. 'Wait!'

Duende froze, the wood still in his hand.

'That's the bronze stick!' Peri explained.

Duende blinked, then squinted at the stick in his hand. 'This?'

Peri reached for the stick. 'Yes. Look at the bark.'

Aziza took the stick to have a closer look. The bark was a shimmering bronze colour. 'You're right,' she said. 'Nice work Peri!' She put the stick in her pocket.

Tiko stared at the fire and shuddered. 'That was a close one.'

Aziza squeezed his furry shoulder. 'But we have it now.'

'We should get going,' Peri said. 'The silvery minute hand is next and that's on Ice Mountain.'

'Do you have to leave so soon?' Duende said. 'I was really enjoying the company and it gets awfully lonely in here.'

Aziza thought for a moment. 'Why don't you go back to town? Everyone will still be at the fete.'

'I'm not sure . . .' Duende said hesitantly. He glanced around his cave. 'It's so snuggly and warm here!'

'You should go,' Aziza assured him. 'You'll have so much fun.'

'You're right! Sometimes I think you can get too used to staying inside.'

They left the cave and waved Duende off.

Peri shot up into the sky once more.

'To Ice Mountain, she cried. 'It isn't far.'

Tiko transformed back into a Sarimanok
and joined her, followed by Aziza and Otis
with Hainu cradled in his arms.

'Do you think we'll see Anka and Ccoa?' Tiko asked as they flew through the sky.

'Who's Cocoa?' Otis asked, wobbling slightly in the sky.

'Ccoa,' Aziza repeated. 'He's a magical Ice Cat and he belongs to Anka, the sorcerer that lives on the mountain.'

Otis dipped lower in the sky as he tried to find the perfect rhythm for his wings.

'What's the matter?' Aziza asked.

'There are so many people in Shimmerton. What if we don't find the sticks in time?' Otis dipped again. 'What

if I ruin Shimmerton on my very first visit?

Jamal Justice would never just turn up in

a place and ruin it. He would be helpful.

He'd be a hero!'

'Uh-oh. He's losing his happy thought,' Peri cried.

Aziza dropped down beside Otis. 'You have to stop worrying.'

Otis flapped his wings frantically. 'How?'

'Think about all the amazing things you've seen and people you've met,' Aziza replied. Hainu nuzzled his nose into Otis's arm. 'You even have a dog now and you're doing a great job of looking after him.'

Otis smiled. 'I am, aren't I?'

Immediately he shot back up into the air. Aziza joined him with a sigh of relief. Soon Ice

Mountain came into view. Its snow-covered peak loomed like a mighty rock giant.

'Brrr.' Peri shivered, tugging at her short sleeves. 'It's a bit chilly.'

'Isn't that Ccoa?' cried Tiko, pointing towards the mountain.

Aziza peered through the clouds and saw the grey Ice Cat slinking up the rocky path. *If he's here, Anka must be close by.*

The four friends descended quickly, landing behind the Ice Cat. Ccoa sniffed the air and turned just as Tiko transformed back to his regular form. Ccoa's black stripes shimmered and his glowing eyes sparked from the hail falling from them. The cat growled softly and Aziza and her friends froze.

But Hainu wasn't fazed. He bounded up beside Ccoa and began sniffing him.

'Oh, look, Hainu's being friendly,' Otis exclaimed.

Aziza hoped Ccoa was feeling friendly too. Hainu was licking Ccoa's face and the cat happily let him. Then

Ccoa straightened and bounded onto a path that wound up the mountain.

Peri strode forward. 'We should follow him.'

They did, and soon they reached a magnificent stone temple near the peak of the mountain. At the entrance stood a tall woman wearing a brightly coloured robe and a golden headdress. There was a worried look on her face, but it disappeared the instant she saw Ccoa.

'Where have you been?' Anka chided softly. When she spotted Aziza and her friends, her hazel eyes lit up. 'Oh, you brought me some guests. Come in, come in.'

Ccoa padded off in the opposite direction to a tall stone pillar and began pawing at it, as if it was a scratching post. Hainu followed and joined in, trying to copy the cat's movements.

Anka laughed. 'I think your magic puppy wants to stay out here with my magic cat.'

'It's ok. I'll stay and watch Hainu,' Otis offered eagerly. 'He's my responsibility.'

Anka nodded and led the others inside the temple, where Aziza explained their quest to her. The walls were covered in colourful gems and golden stars, and shiny crystals hung from the ceiling. Patterned ceramic bowls lined the edges of the stone floor, and in the centre of the room was a huge cauldron. There was nothing wooden in sight, and definitely no sticks.

Crack!

The thunderous sound echoed across the room and Aziza heard Tiko give a loud cry.

Chapter 6

Aziza whirled round. 'Are you OK, Tiko?'

Tiko rubbed at one of his furry ears. 'I wish I didn't have such good hearing! What was that?'

Anka frowned. 'I think it was thunder.

A storm must be on its way.

'Oh no!' Aziza cried. 'Otis is still outside with Hainu and Ccoa. It could be dangerous.'

Aziza raced outside, with Tiko, Anka and Peri close behind her. She really hoped Otis was alright. There they found Hainu and Ccoa leaping over one another. Otis stood nearby, with a shocked look on his face.

'Just so you know. This is definitely not my fault,' Otis said.

Aziza frowned. 'What isn't?'

Before Otis could reply, Ccoa rolled onto his back and playfully batted at Hainu's face.

The
puppy
jumped
aside and
let out a
thunderous bark. It
echoed across the mountain and then came
an answering growl from the sky.

'That!' Otis said, pointing at Hainu. 'They
were playing. Then suddenly he started doing
that!'

Glittersticks! The thunder is coming from
Hainu, Aziza realized. *That must be what*

Mr Bracken meant about his bark.

Suddenly a shaft of bright light streaked across the sky, lighting up the mountaintop like a bright, whizzing firework. Tiko squeaked, curling up into a small ball.

Aziza gasped. 'Is Hainu making lightning as well?'

'My mum says you can't have thunder without lightning.' Tiko said, his voice muffled by his furry legs.

'Is it me or is it getting colder?' Otis said, shivering.

Tiko unfurled himself and Aziza noticed

that a thin layer of ice had begun to coat everything.

'It's Ccoa,' Anka said gently. 'When he gets upset or has other big emotions, it causes frost and even hailstones to form.'

'S-seriously?' Otis replied, his teeth chattering. 'Pets in Shimmerton are kind of different to the ones you get at home!'

Tiko eyed the darkening sky with troubled eyes. 'You don't think this storm will end up in Shimmerton, do you?'

Peri bit her lip. 'It looks like it could.'

'We need to calm Hainu and

Ccoa down.' Aziza said.

Otis approached the excited pets and tried to pick up Hainu, but Ccoa growled, sending Otis scuttling backwards.

'Any other ideas?' he asked.

'I think I have just the thing,' said Anka. She went back inside and emerged with a saucer full of shimmering milk.

'Ccoa,' she called in a soothing voice.

The cat lifted his head and sniffed the air. Then he bounded over and began to drink.

'Full-moon milk,' Anka explained. Almost immediately, the ice around them began to thaw.

'Look,' Otis cried. 'He's calming down.'

Peri wriggled her fingers. 'And it's getting warmer.'

Unhappy with being left out, Hainu padded over to his new friend and sniffed at the milk curiously.

Otis frowned. 'Is it safe for puppies?'

'I can't imagine why not,' Anka said.

She coaxed Hainu closer and soon the puppy was slurping away happily. As the two pets drank their fill, the dark clouds cleared, replaced by a clear pink sky. *It's a good thing Anka was here*, Aziza thought. The sorcerer was really smart. An idea came to her.

'Do you think you could use your magic to help us find the silver stick – the missing minute hand?' she asked the sorcerer.

Anka tapped her chin thoughtfully. 'I could try a special finders-keepers potion.'

'Oh, yes please,' Tiko said, bouncing with excitement.

'But it will take a little time,' Anka warned. Aziza felt her tummy twist with worry. 'Why don't you and your friends keep searching the mountain? Who knows, maybe you'll find it before I'm done.' Then Anka turned and called to Ccoa. 'Come my sweet. We've got to find some horsetail weed. Then I just need to remember where I left my other herbs.'

Aziza, Otis and their friends set off to search the mountain. They looked in between mossy nooks and rough crannies but found no trace of the silver stick. Until at last they came across the open mouth of a big cave.

'We should check inside,' Peri suggested.

'The last cave we went into had hot chocolate,' Otis said. 'So I'm totally on board with that idea.'

Aziza laughed, but as they entered the cave she realized it was very different from Duende's home. It was dark and smelly and they had barely entered when they heard the sound of voices. Peeping around the corner, Aziza saw a group of men with rosy cheeks and pointy hats arguing. Suddenly one of the

men jumped back and waved something in the air. It was a shiny silver stick. *Glittersticks! It's the minute hand!*

Then the man flung the stick. It whistled through the air and landed in an old boot a few paces away. *Are they playing hoopla with it?* she wondered in horror. *I'm glad the Zorigami's not here to see this.*

'Quick! hide,' Peri whispered frantically.

They all ducked behind a large boulder.

'Who are they?' Otis asked, confused.

'Yule Lads,' Tiko replied with a grim look. 'They like to cause trouble in winter unless we leave them treats.'

'They're a menace,' Peri shuddered. 'Always playing nasty tricks and leaving rotten potatoes about.'

Aziza straightened. 'Well, we need that stick. We just need to figure out how to get it back.'

'You can't just take it, Zizi! Otis said. 'I'm sure if we explained everything, they'd be happy to help. It's what Jamal Justice would do.'

'Um, Otis—,'

But Otis wasn't listening. Leaving their

hiding place, he quickly jogged over to the group of men. The magic puppy ran by his side.

'A bit impulsive, isn't he?' Peri grumbled. 'I mean, he could have at least waited for us to come up with a plan.'

Aziza laughed.

'What?' Peri said crossing her arms. Aziza gave her a knowing look.

Peri grimaced. 'Me!' she exclaimed. 'I'm not that bad.'

Tiko coughed. 'We really shouldn't leave him to deal with the Yule Lads on his own.'

The trio scrambled after Otis, who had stepped a bit closer to the Yule Lad who held the stick.

'That's Pot Scraper,' Peri whispered. 'He likes to steal dirty pots so he can lick them clean.'

'Hey! Stop!' Otis called out. 'That stick doesn't belong to you.'

Pot Scraper lifted a bushy eyebrow. 'Says who?' Then he turned the stick over. 'I don't see your name on it.'

Otis frowned. 'You don't even know my name.'

'I still don't see it here.'

'Yeah,' replied a different Yule Lad. 'We found it fair and square.'

'Look, it's not really a stick,' Aziza said standing at her brother's side. 'It's part of the Shimmerton town clock and we need it. Otherwise, spring will be paused.'

Pot Scraper examined the silver stick even more closely. 'Valuable is it? Well, we don't care about spring not springing. We like it cold. Yes we do.'

Aziza frowned. 'But nothing will grow.'

'We don't like things growing neither.'

Peri stepped forward. 'But you do love games, don't you?' Then she pointed to the old boot. She smiled innocently. 'Hoopla, right?'

Pot Scraper looked at Peri suspiciously. 'Yeah, what of it?'

'Tell you what,' Peri said. 'I challenge you to a game of hoopla. If I win you lot have to give the stick back.'

'And when I win?' Pot Scraper asked cheekily.

'You can keep it and anything else you choose.'

'The puppy. I want the puppy,' cried a Yule Lad.

'What do you need a puppy for, Gully Gawk?' Pot Scraper said. 'Don't you remember what happened to the last pet you had?'

'How was I to know five pies was five pies too many?' Gully Gawk complained. 'I promise I'll do better this time.'

Pot Scraper thought for a minute. 'Huddle!' he yelled.

The Yule Lads clustered together in a tight circle and began to mutter quietly.

Otis pulled Hainu into his arms. 'Nah, mate. There's no way I'm giving him up.'

'It's ok,' Peri whispered. 'You won't have to. I'm brilliant at hoopla. Never lost a game.'

Tiko's nose twitched. 'Erm, Peri, that's not strictly true.'

Peri waved Tiko's words away. Then seeing Otis's worried face, she squeezed his shoulder. 'I promise, I can do this.'

At last the muttering stopped and Pot Scraper turned around.

'Alright then. Challenge accepted.'

Chapter 7

Pot Scraper stared at Aziza, Tiko, Peri and Otis with a sly look. 'One more thing, we've decided it'll be more fun if we play four of us against you lot.'

'What? But that wasn't the deal,'

Peri spluttered.

'What's the matter, little fairy? Scared you and your friends are gonna lose?'

Peri straightened to her full height. 'Of course not.'

Pot Scraper smiled. 'Good. The rules are simple. Each thrower has to stand ten paces back from the boot and they've got ten seconds to make their throw.'

Aziza felt a knot tighten in her stomach. 'I'm not sure about this.'

'Neither am I,' Tiko said. 'What if I miss?'

Peri patted him on the shoulder.

'It'll be fine. You'll see.'

Aziza sighed. The whole plan felt too risky. She looked at her brother and saw that he looked sick.

'You OK, Otis?'

'What if I fail?' He muttered. 'There's a lot riding on this and I don't want to mess it up.'

'Riding!' Tiko exclaimed. 'That's a brilliant idea.'

Then he shut his eyes, scrunched up his nose and disappeared. When he reappeared, he was a magnificent centaur that towered over everyone. He had the torso of a man with the body and legs of a horse. Tiko swished

his long tail and Hainu jumped up, trying to

grab it.

'Erm, Tiko,' Aziza began. 'How is that going to help?'

Tiko stamped his front hooves. 'Centaurs are brilliant archers. They have the best aim.'

'Oi, that's not fair,' Pot Scraper grumbled as he bustled over. 'You can't just be shape-shifting all over the place.'

'There's nothing in the rules that says we can't.' Peri replied. 'You can use magic too if you want.'

'Harumph,' grumped Pot Scraper. 'As if we have any.'

Peri shrugged. 'My dad says you should

always play to your strengths.'

'Well, we can play that game too, missy.'
Pot Scraper beckoned to a Yule Lad with
great big muscles. 'Door Slammer, you're
up.'

Aziza shared a look with Peri and Tiko
but said nothing as Door Slammer took his
place ten paces away from the boot. Then,
with a mighty roar, he flung the stick.
It whizzed through the air like a rocket,
soaring past the boot until it smacked into
the cave wall with a thud. Pot Scraper
glared at Door Slammer who darted back

and hid behind Gully Gawk.

'My turn,' Peri cried with glee.

She retrieved the stick then confidently stepped into position. With a careful flick, Peri threw the stick. It soared away in a glorious arc and landed in the boot like they were long lost friends.

'Woohoo!' Peri crowed. 'We're winning.'

Aziza felt the knot in her belly ease. *Maybe we can do this.* Then up stepped a Yule Lad with a link of pink sausages wrapped around his neck.

'Come on, Sausage Swiper,' Gully Gawk

said. 'Do it for the Lads.'

With total ease, Sausage Swiper sent the stick into the boot with a perfect toss. He then did a victory dance with his lasso of sausages.

'It's enough to put you off your lunch,' Otis muttered. Hainu still looked peckish.

It was Tiko's turn next. He cantered into place, his tail swishing behind him. But just as he went to throw the stick, his tail flicked up and hit the side of his head. Tiko gave a whinny of surprise and reared up on his hind legs. The stick tumbled from his hand and hit the hard ground.

'Ha!' cried Pot Scraper. 'That's your turn gone.'

Tiko's head dropped as he trotted back to his friends.

'I'm so sorry,' he mumbled. 'It's really hard when your bottom half won't listen to the top half.' His tail flicked the air again.

'It's okay, Tiko,' Peri assured him. 'You tried your best and that's all you can do.'

'Tell you what,' called Pot Scraper with a smirk. 'Since I'm feeling so generous, you go next. Try and claim a point back.'

He pointed the stick towards Otis, who

swallowed. As if sensing his nerves, Hainu

gave his hand a gentle lick.

'You can do it,' Aziza told her brother.

'Just think of Jamal Justice. He always saves

the day, but only because he concentrates
and finds the power inside him.'

Otis nodded and took his place. Aziza
closed one eye as Otis released the stick.

'Yes!' she cried, jumping with excitement when it landed perfectly.

'Thanks, sis,' Otis said with a wide grin. 'I couldn't have done it without you.'

One of the Yule Lads grabbed the stick, looked at it hungrily and gave it a lick.

'Spoon Licker!' Pot Scraper yelled, his hands on his hips. 'How many times have I told you. It's a stick not a spoon.'

'But it looks a bit like a spoon,' Spoon Licker said. 'It's so shiny.'

'Well it's not. You're supposed to throw it.'

Spoon Licker scratched his head and stared

longingly at the stick. 'Do I have to?'

Pot Scraper rolled his eyes. 'You're hopeless, you know that.'

'Disqualified!' Peri crowed. 'It's been more than ten seconds,'

By now, Spoon Licker had shoved the stick into his mouth and was happily slurping away. *Eww,* Aziza thought. *I've still got to throw that.*

Pot Scraper sighed. 'Fine, whatever. We can still win this. Candle Stealer, you take your turn.' Then he turned back to Aziza and her friends, a smug grin on his lips.

'He's the best, anyway.'

Peri gulped.

Candle Stealer stepped up and, with a small wriggle of his bottom, he hurled the stick. Aziza held her breath as it sailed through the air.

'Please don't go in,' Aziza whispered under her breath.

But the stick shot into the boot, straight and true. The Yule Lads let out a loud whoop of victory.

'Told you,' Pot Scraper crowed triumphantly. 'Beat that.'

Aziza swallowed. It was all down to her now.

'You can do it too, sis,' Otis whispered.

Peri and Tiko nodded, their expressions full of encouragement. Aziza closed her eyes. *I can do this. My friends believe in me. So does my brother.*

Then she got into position, took a deep breath and launched the stick at the boot. It whistled through the air, then began to drift slightly to the left.

'No, no, no,' Aziza muttered under her breath.

Then suddenly the stick corrected itself before landing with a gentle thud inside the boot. Aziza punched the sky and did her own victory dance.

'We did it!' Otis cried, scooping Hainu into his arms and giving him a big hug.

Peri marched up to Pot Scraper.

'Now hand over that stick.'

'Make us!' Pot Scraper said as the Yule Lads clustered protectively behind him.

Chapter 8

A thunderous growl filled the air as Hainu bared his teeth at the Yule Lads. They scrambled, almost falling backwards over themselves.

'On second thoughts, you did win fair

and square,' Pot Scraper said as he shoved the silver stick into Aziza's hand. 'You guys really should get going now.'

The other Yule Lads nodded eagerly.

'Why don't you go into town and join the fete?' Aziza suggested, suddenly feeling sorry for them. The Yule Lads weren't that bad after all, and they all looked terrified. 'There are loads more games and it'll be more fun than hanging around here.'

Pot Scraper eyed her suspiciously. 'We'll think about it. Not making any promises, mind you.'

'Suit yourselves,' Peri replied. 'We're off to the river anyway.'

Tiko reared up onto his hind legs. 'I think I've got the hang of this centaur thing. I'll meet you there.'

Then off he galloped out of the cave at lightning speed.

'Look,' Otis cried when he and the others finally exited the cave.

The sun was now nearing the horizon, casting a dappled orange glow over the pink sky.

Aziza frowned. 'I hope it won't take too

long to find the last stick. It will be sunset soon.'

By the time they arrived at the river, Tiko was back to his usual self, but he wasn't alone. Beside him was a pretty girl in a colourful dress with her arms raised. Multicoloured braids hung down her back in a glorious burst of colours that matched the rainbow bridge forming across the fast-flowing river.

'It's Resa!' Peri called, waving hard. 'That bridge looks awesome.'

'Nice rainbow,' Otis said with a grin. 'How are you doing that?'

Resa gave a shy smile. 'I'm a Rainbow Maker.'

'The youngest ever in Shimmerton,' Peri added.

Hainu could not resist the rainbow bridge and dashed over to it. As he scampered across, his fur began to change colour. It transformed from white to a brilliant red.

'Wow, that's amazing,' Otis breathed.

Hainu bounded to the middle of

the bridge and this time his fur shimmered a glorious yellow. He started to chase his tail. As he did his fur took on every hue of the rainbow.

Aziza was pleased the puppy was having fun, but time was ticking.

'Resa, you haven't seen a gold-coloured stick around by any chance?' Aziza asked.

Resa shook her head.

'I already asked,' Tiko said, looking a bit down.

'Sorry,' Resa added. 'I've been busy practising my rainbow, but I can help you look.'

Peri threw back her shoulders determinedly.

'I guess we should —'

'Swoop in and save the day,' interrupted a voice from above.

Aziza looked up just as the Gigglers landed with a chorus of giggles. 'Miss us?' Kendra asked.

'What are you doing here?' Peri demanded. 'I thought finding the sticks was too much work for you.'

Kendra smirked back. 'Yeah, but you've done most of the work now, haven't you?'

'Haven't you?' Felly echoed. Kendra gave her a high five.

'You lot are so predictable,' Kendra continued. 'We knew you'd find the first two sticks.'

Noon tossed her head. 'And now we'll find the last one. We'll be totally heroic.'

Peri's eyes narrowed. 'This is just like you

Gigglers. Leave us to do the work and then try and swipe the glory.'

'But you could do with some extra eyes, right?' Kendra asked.

Peri sighed. Tiko shrugged. Aziza wasn't happy about the Gigglers' sudden appearance but they were running out of time and the sun was close to setting.

'We could do with the help,' Aziza admitted.

Otis looked less convinced, but before he could say anything Kendra pointed towards the grassy bank on the other side of the river.

'OMG. What's that?'

Aziza squinted. A small glint caught her eye.
It was a golden stick, lodged in the ground.

'I'll get it.' Peri zoomed into the sky.

'No, I will.' Kendra raced after her.

Peri and Kendra landed at the exact same
moment, each reaching for the stick.

'Let go,' Kendra demanded.

Peri yanked on the stick. 'No, you let go.'

'I got here first.' Kendra tugged harder.

'You did not,' Peri grunted.

Otis shook his head. 'I have a bad feeling about this.'

Aziza huffed in frustration as she watched the two fairies. *We don't have time for this.*

Suddenly the golden stick shot into the air, soaring over the squabble. *Oh no,* Aziza thought. *Not the river.* She watched as the stick flew into the choppy water and began to bob away.

'Now look what you did,' Kendra jeered.

'Me?' Peri exclaimed. 'You're the one who wouldn't let go.'

'It doesn't matter,' Aziza yelled. 'Someone save that stick.'

Before either Peri or Kendra could take flight again, a loud yelp sounded from the rainbow bridge. Then, with a mighty splash, Hainu leapt into the water and was paddling hard towards the stick.

'Go, Hainu!' Otis whooped. The puppy reached the

stick, grabbing it in his mouth, then paddled back to the riverbank. The others raced to greet him. Hainu clambered out with a great big shake, sending water in every direction and soaking them all.

'Eww,' Kendra whined. 'I smell like wet magic puppy.'

Otis barely noticed as he bent and scooped up the little dog. 'You did it, Hainu.' He gave the puppy a big squeeze. 'Who's a good boy?'

Aziza took the two other sticks from her pocket, and Otis handed her the third one.

'We need to get all three sticks back to the

fete.' Aziza looked up at the darkening sky. 'Fast.'

Peri winked. 'The fastest way to travel in Shimmerton is wing power.'

She shot up into the air, the Gigglers close behind her. Tiko twitched his nose, transformed back into the Sarimanok and joined the others. Aziza nodded to her brother and together they lifted off, with Hainu circling close. Together the group raced towards the fete. But Otis was struggling to keep up with the others.

'We'll never get there in time at this rate,

with Mr Slow Wings holding us up,' Kendra
grumbled.

Peri gave her a sharp look. 'He's literally
only just learnt how to fly. Give him a break.'

'I just tell it like I see it,' Kendra replied.

'She's right, guys, I am slowing you down.'

Otis shooed them away. 'Go on without me. You'll get there quicker. Besides, I've got Hainu to keep me company.'

'Are you sure, Otis?' Aziza asked.

'I'm more than sure,' Otis said. 'Go ahead and give back those sticks. The whole of Shimmerton should know about what you and your friends have done today.'

'What we've done, Otis,' Aziza said. She turned to Peri. 'Take these,' she said, handing over the three sticks. 'I'll stay with Otis while you get them back to the Zorigami.'

'But—' Peri began.

'You heard her,' Kendra said. 'Let's go.'

Aziza rolled her eyes as the Gigglers zoomed off without a backward glance. Tiko twitched his nose.

'You've got to hurry!' Aziza cried. With one final look at Aziza and Otis, Tiko and Peri sped away too.

'Do you think they'll make it?' Otis asked.

Aziza stared after her friends, now just a dot in the distance.

'I hope so.'

Chapter 9

By the time Otis and Aziza arrived at the fete, there was just a sliver of sunlight peeping over the horizon. Twinkling fairy lights lit up the stalls, like playful fireflies.

'I really hope they made it,' Otis said as

he bent over to pat Hainu. He was breathing

hard from all the flying.

'There's only one way to find out.'

They quickly made their way to the town

clock, where a large crowd had gathered to

see its second unveiling. The Zorigami stood

behind the king and queen, ready to pull the

velvet cloth away.

Aziza spotted Peri and Tiko in the crowd. She and Otis went to join them.

'You made it just in time,' Peri said with a grin. 'I knew you would.'

'Thank you, ladies and gentlemen,' the Zorigami tick-tocked. Silence fell over the crowd. 'May I once again present the spring clock.'

It was almost silent, as if the whole crowd were holding their breath, as the Zorigami whipped the cloth away to reveal the clock. Only this time, all three hands shone from their resting place inside the clock face. Then the Zorigami glanced around with a worried look on his face.

'What's the matter?' Aziza asked.

'It's not ticking.' Peri bit her thumb. 'It's supposed to ti—,'

Before she could finish, the bronze second hand began to move and the soft sound of ticking filled the air. It was followed by a huge bang as coloured fairy dust exploded from a secret compartment nestled in the top of the clock. It rained down in a fabulous shower of beautiful colours. *It's so pretty,* thought Aziza. *It looks like the red dust from the*

Holi festival we read about in school. Beside her, Peri breathed a huge sigh of relief as the crowd roared their delight.

'Oh, I'm so glad you didn't miss it,' Peri cried. 'It's my favourite part of the whole fete.'

'Spring has finally sprung,' Tiko added, as he twirled in the colourful dust.

The Zorigami bustled up to the four friends. 'I believe congratulations are in order.'

Otis looked at him, surprised. 'You're not angry anymore?'

'While I'd prefer it if you stayed away from

my work in future, I'm rather impressed with your teamwork. It couldn't have been easy getting all those pieces back in time. I should know.' The Zorigami frowned. 'You should probably keep that troublesome puppy on a tight leash though.'

'Actually, we couldn't have done it without Hainu,' Otis replied.

Tiko nodded. 'He saved the final stick. He's a hero.'

'I would thank him myself, but I can't see him anywhere.' The Zorigami winked and shuffled away.

'Oh no, not again,' Otis groaned. 'Hainu!'

'Where could he be?' Peri said.

Otis looked around, a frantic expression on his face. 'I really hope he's not messing with the clock again.'

'Hello,' said a familiar voice. Aziza spun round and saw Anka coming up behind the group. 'I've finished that finders-keepers potion, though it doesn't look like you'll be needing it.'

'Actually,' Aziza said with a worried look. 'I think we do. We can't find Hainu.'

Anka pulled out a small bottle from her robe

and opened it. Almost immediately, a thin tendril of smoke swirled out of it and settled in the air in the shape of a small arrow. A moment later the arrow began to move, drifting through the crowd of people.

'I suggest you follow that arrow,' Anka said softly.

With a cry of thanks, Aziza, Otis, Peri and Tiko dashed after it. Aziza spotted Duende, having tea with Tiko's mum by the cake stall, as she ran. Then a flash of red caught her eye. It was Door Slammer, playing the strength tester game.

Suddenly the arrow stopped, right above the Gigglers . . . and a very playful Hainu.

They were playing fetch with a ball and each time they threw it, Hainu would leap up and catch it mid-air.

'He looks really happy,' Otis said quietly.

Aziza looked at her brother. 'I know you love Hainu, and I care about him too, but we really can't take him home.'

Otis sighed. 'I know.'

'I'd offer to take care of him,' Peri said, 'but my dad's allergic to dogs.'

Tiko nodded. 'So would I, but our den's just not big enough.'

'Same with our flat,' Otis said. 'He'd be

miserable there, I see that now.'

'I'll take him,' Kendra strode up to the four friends, Hainu, Noon and Felly close behind her.

Peri shook her head. 'Eavesdropping, again?'

Kendra stuck her tongue out at Peri. 'I've always wanted a pet.' Then she turned to Felly and Noon. 'You guys will help too, won't you?'

'Totally,' Felly said.

Noon clapped her hands. 'We'd love to.'

'You can always come back and visit him

whenever you want.' Then Kendra eyed Aziza. 'I guess you can bring her too.'

Aziza rolled her eyes, but a part of her knew this was the right thing for Hainu. *The Gigglers really are great with him.*

'Shouldn't you check with your parents first?' Peri asked.

Kendra's face scrunched up. 'Why? They'll only say yes.'

Felly threw Noon a hesitant look.

'Still, we should probably check,' Felly finally said. 'Remember what happened with the porcupine?'

★

'Of course, my little Kendra-kins can have a puppy,' Kendra's dad cooed. 'You know you can have anything you want.'

'Nothing's too good for our little princesses.' Felly's mum glanced at Peri. 'No offence, your highness.'

'No wonder the Gigglers act the way they do,' Peri whispered to Aziza. 'They're spoiled rotten.'

'Although,' began Noon's dad, pushing his thick glasses up his nose. 'You'll need to look after him properly.'

Kendra's mum, a little fairy with a big voice nodded. 'Pets are a huge responsibility. Don't think I've forgotten about the porcupine.'

Kendra blushed. 'Yes, Mummy. I promise to be a responsible pet owner. Look.' She pointed at Hainu. 'Sit!'

Immediately the puppy dropped to his bottom and so did Felly, making everyone laugh.

Peri looked at Aziza. 'Now we've fixed the clock, it's time for you to go isn't it?'

Aziza nodded sadly.

'It was great meeting you, Otis,' Tiko said.

With hugs goodbye and promises to return soon, Aziza and Otis took to the air one last time in search of the fairy door. They didn't need to look very hard, as the soft shimmery glow coming from it guided their way.

'You're getting really good at flying,' Aziza said as they set down.

'I had an amazing teacher,' Otis replied. 'Today was incredible, Zizi. Thanks for sharing Shimmerton with me, even though I was so grumpy with you this morning.'

Aziza shrugged. 'I think I get why you were so upset now. Puppies are awesome.'

'Well, I promise to stop moaning about not having a pet – mum is right about dogs needing lots of space. Maybe a goldfish wouldn't be so bad after all.'

Aziza laughed and together they stepped

through the door. With a flash of light, they

found themselves back in Aziza's room.

Otis and Aziza stared at the fairy door,

now back to its usual size.

'Did all that really just happen?' said Otis.

'Yup,' Aziza replied with a huge grin.

Otis gave his sister a big hug. 'Well, I might not have a pet, but I do have you and you're pretty good at finding sticks.'

Aziza nudged her brother but hugged him back. Then her gaze fell on the fairy door again.

'You know, I never did find out who sent it to me.'

Just then, mum breezed into the room, her face filled with excitement. 'You'll never guess who's coming for a visit.' Mum grinned. 'Great Aunty Az. You're going to love her, Zizzles. She loves fairies almost as much as you.'

Otis snorted. 'I doubt anyone is as keen on fairies as Aziza.'

'Just you wait and see,' Mum said. 'Great Aunty Az is just magic!'

Myths and Legends

Aziza, her friends, and the inhabitants of Shimmerton are inspired by myths and legends from all around the world:

Aziza is named after a type of fairy creature. In West African folklore, specifically *Dahomey mythology*, the Aziza are helpful fairies who live in the forest and are full of wisdom.

Peri's name comes from ancient Persian mythology. Peris are winged spirits who can be kind and helpful, but they also sometimes enjoy playing tricks on people. In paintings they are usually shown with large, bird-like wings.

The Zorigami is based on a Japanese myth about a clock that comes to life after one hundred years.

Duende (pronounced Doo-en-day) is a small, elf-like creature that gets its name from the Spanish word for goblin. Duendes appear in the myths of many other cultures too. Some are helpful. Some are sneaky. Some have magical powers.

Ccoa comes from Peruvian folklore. The ccoa is a cat-like creature and the companion of a mountain god. It can bring about storms, hail and lightning.

Yule Lads are the thirteen merry but mischievous Father Christmases found in Icelandic folklore. Each has a distinct personality. They visit children in the thirteen nights leading up to Christmas.

Resa is based on a South African deity called Mbaba Mwana Waresa. She rules over harvests, agriculture, rain and — of course — rainbows.

Mrs Hattie is a **sphinx**. In Greek and ancient Egyptian mythology, the sphinx is a mythical creature with a human head, a lion's body and large bird wings.

Mrs Sayeed is an **Almiraj**, a legendary rabbit with a unicorn-like horn. They're found in Arabic myths and folklore.

Unicorns have appeared in folklore for thousands of years. Like Mr Bracken, they're normally portrayed as magical, horned white horses and are said to have healing powers.

Phoenixes, like Mr Phoenix, are mystical, bird-like creatures found in Greek mythology. They are said to be immortal and have healing powers.

There are many famous **centaurs** in Greek mythology. They are all half human and half horse.

About the Authors

Lola Morayo is the pen name for the creative partnership of writers Tọ́lá Okogwu and Jasmine Richards.

Tọ́lá is a journalist and author of the *Onyeka and the Academy of the Sun*, and the Daddy Do My Hair series. She is an avid reader who enjoys spending time with her family and friends in her home in Kent, where she lives with her husband and daughters.

© Karen Ball

Jasmine is the founder of an inclusive fiction studio called Storymix and has written more than fifteen books for children, including *The Unmorrow Curse*. She lives in Hertfordshire with her husband and two children.

Both are passionate about telling stories that are inclusive and joyful.

About the Illustrator

© Katarina Tibenska

Cory Reid lives in Kettering and is an illustrator and designer who has worked in the creative industry for more than fifteen years, with clients including Usborne Publishing, Owlet Press and Card Factory.